# The Midnight Circus

*PETER COLLINGTON*

ALFRED A. KNOPF · NEW YORK

*This is a Borzoi Book published by Alfred A. Knopf, Inc.*
Copyright © 1992 by Peter Collington
All rights reserved under International and Pan-American Copyright Conventions. Published in the United States by Alfred A. Knopf, Inc., New York. Distributed by Random House, Inc., New York. Originally published in Great Britain in 1992 by Heinemann Young Books. Manufactured in Italy    1  2  3  4  5  6  7  8  9  10

Library of Congress Cataloging-in-Publication Data
Collington, Peter. The midnight circus / by Peter Collington.   p.   cm. Summary: A young boy's favorite mechanical horse comes to life and carries him to a circus for a night of adventure and stardom.
ISBN: 0-679-83262-9 (trade)   ISBN: 0-679-93262-3 (lib. bdg.)
[1. Circus—Fiction. 2. Horses—Fiction. 3. Toys—Fiction. 4. Stories without words.]
I. Title   PZ7.C686Mi  1992   [E]—dc20   91-39535

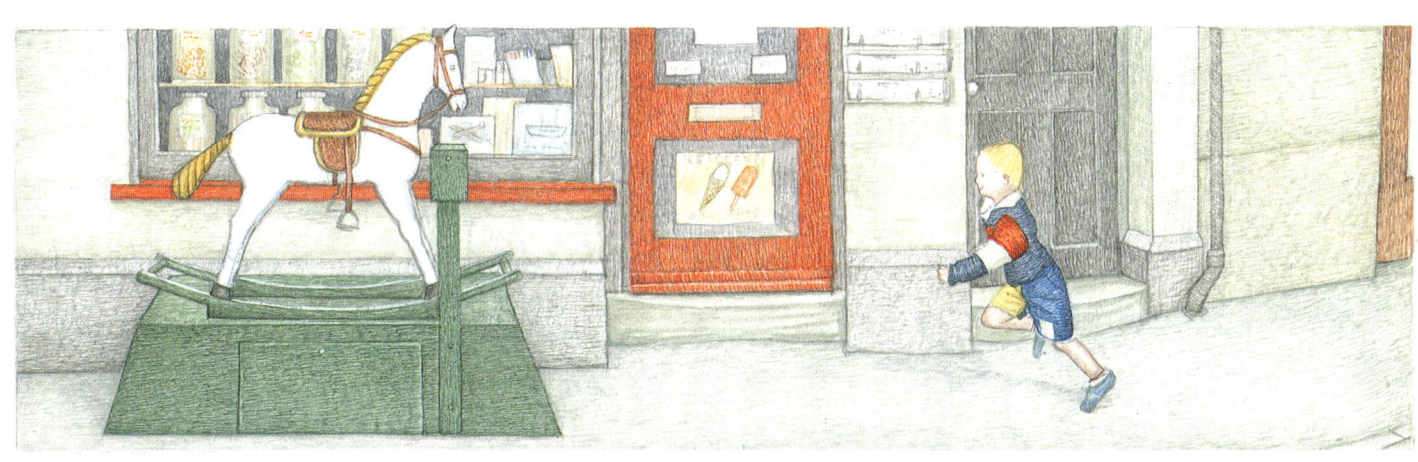

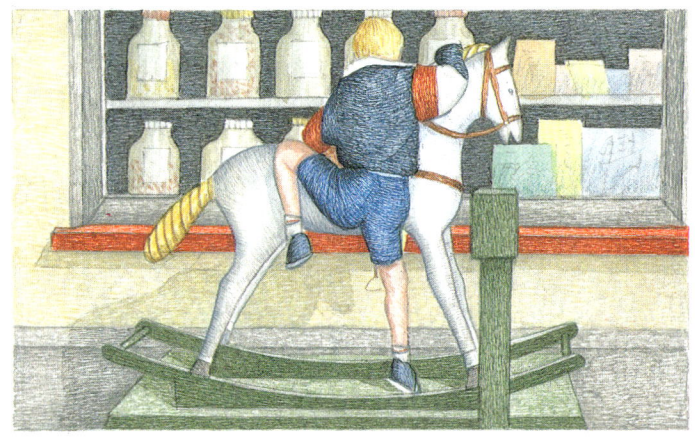

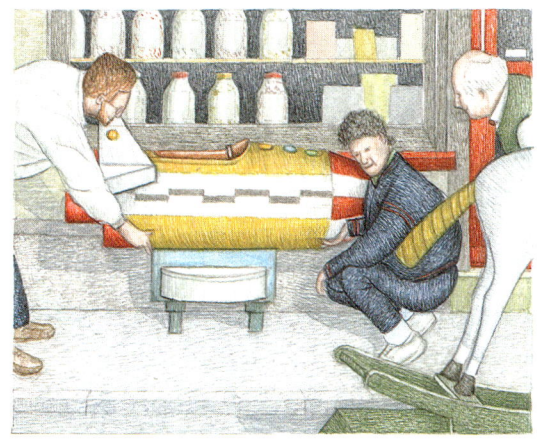

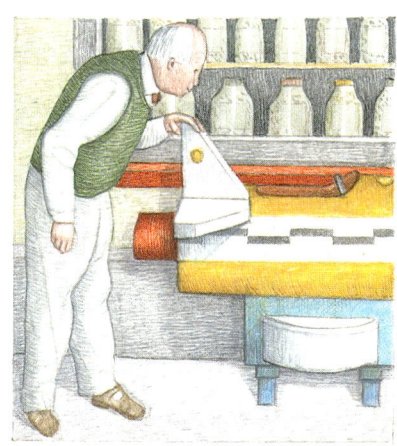

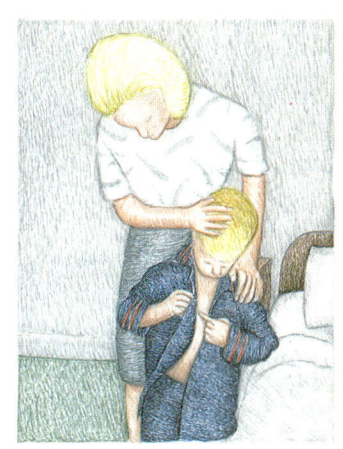
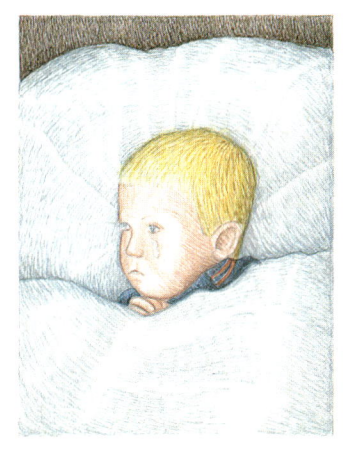

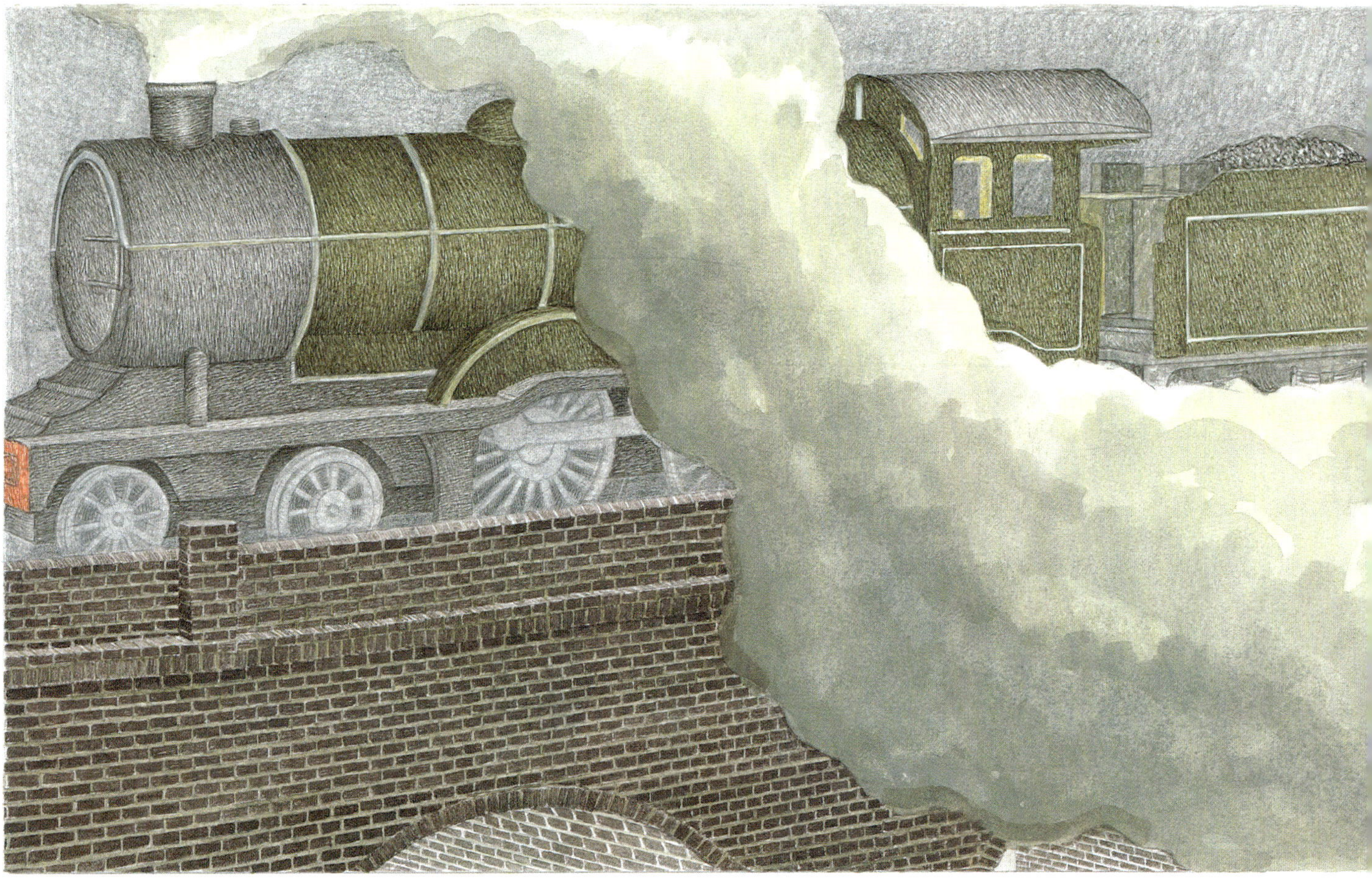

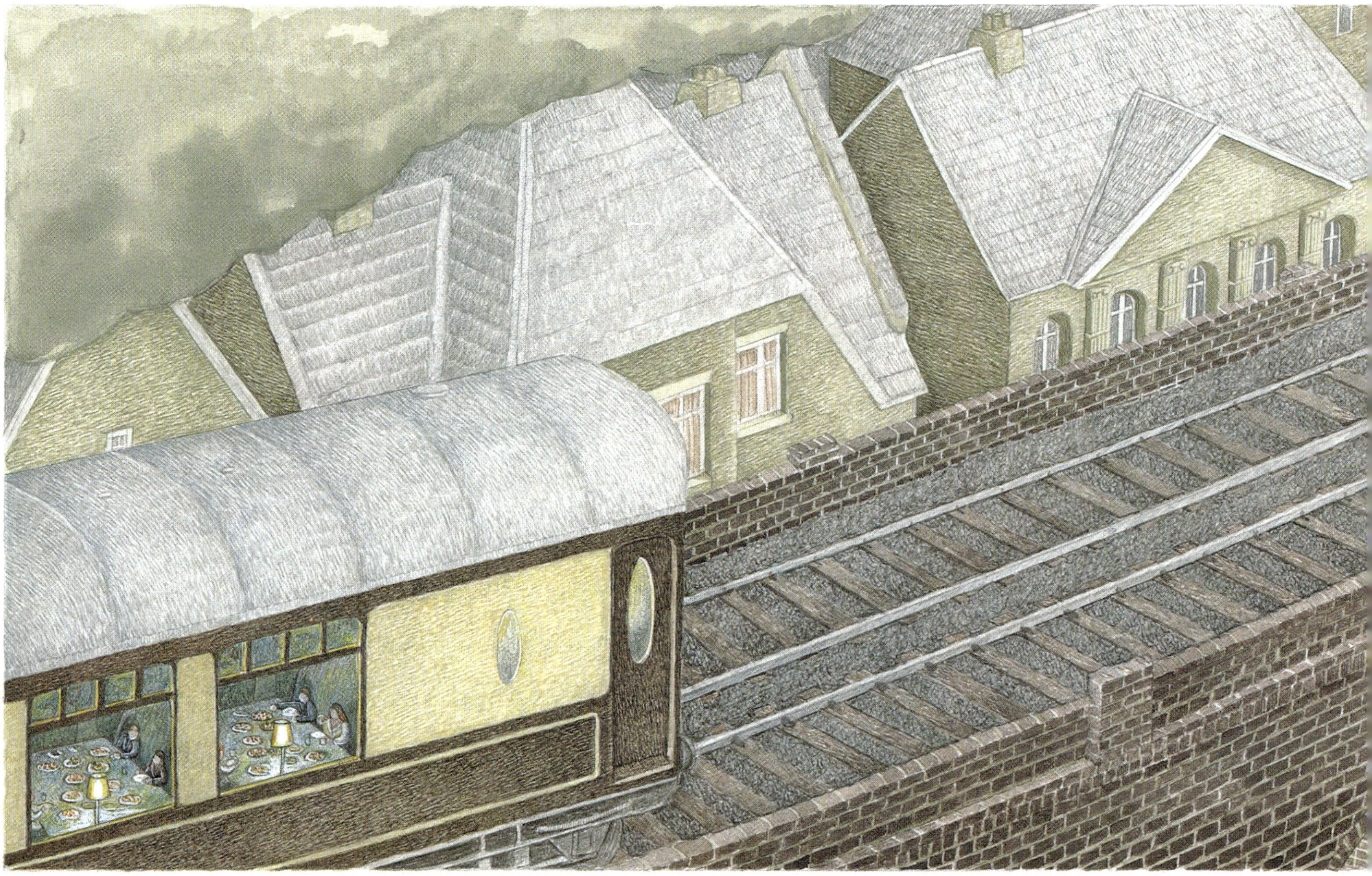

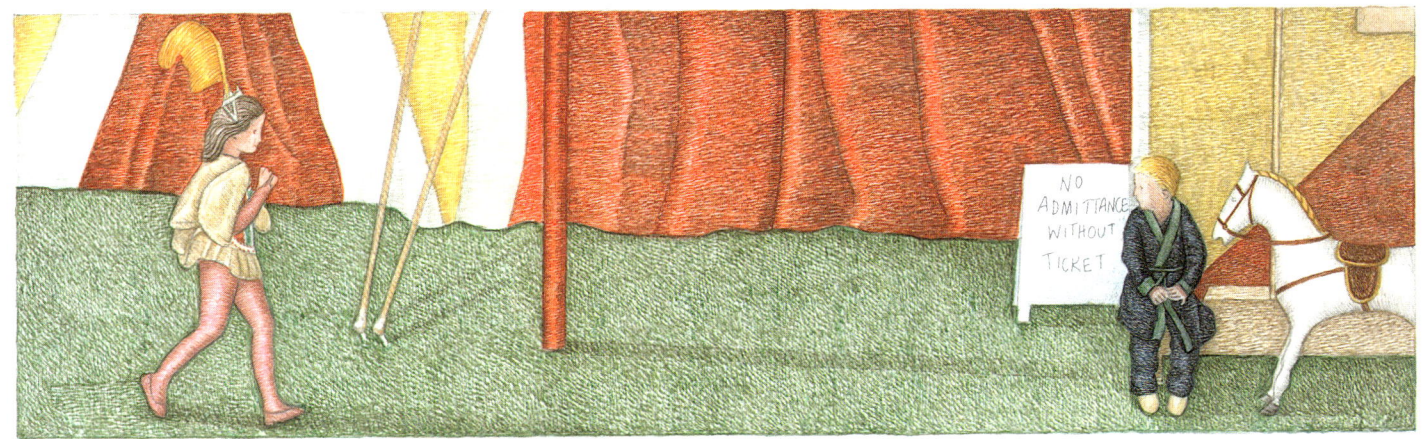

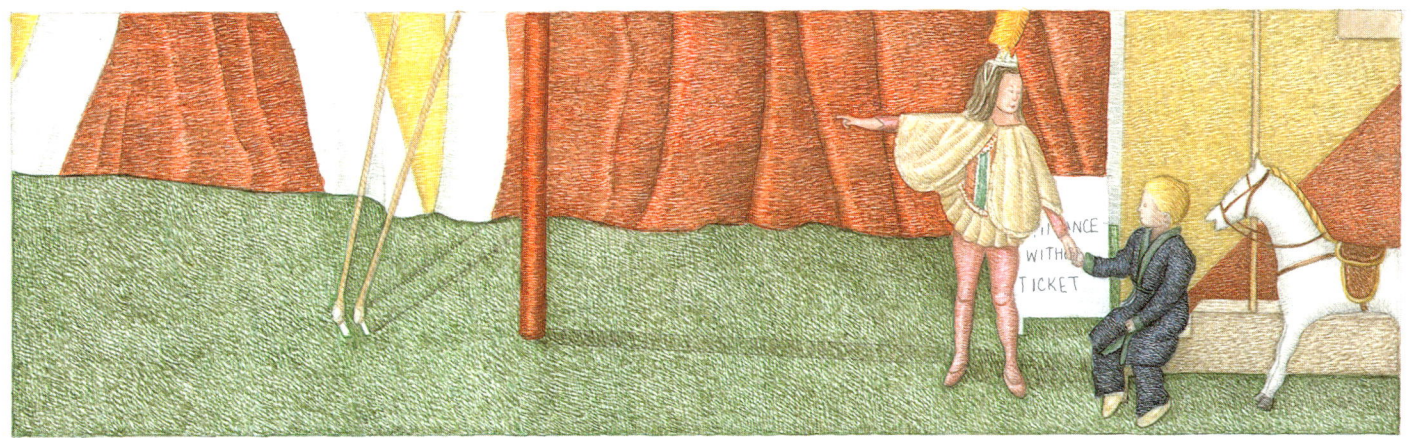

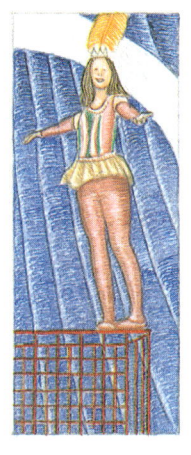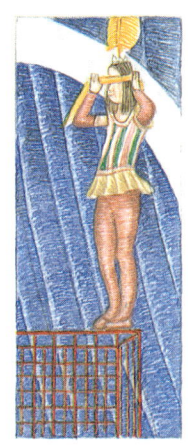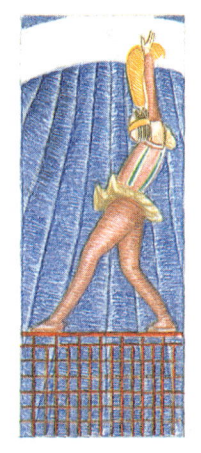

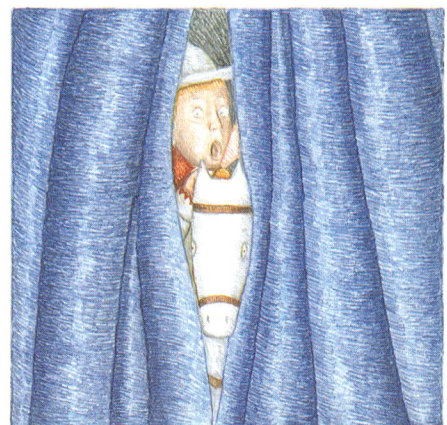

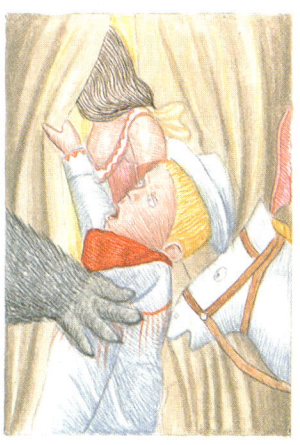

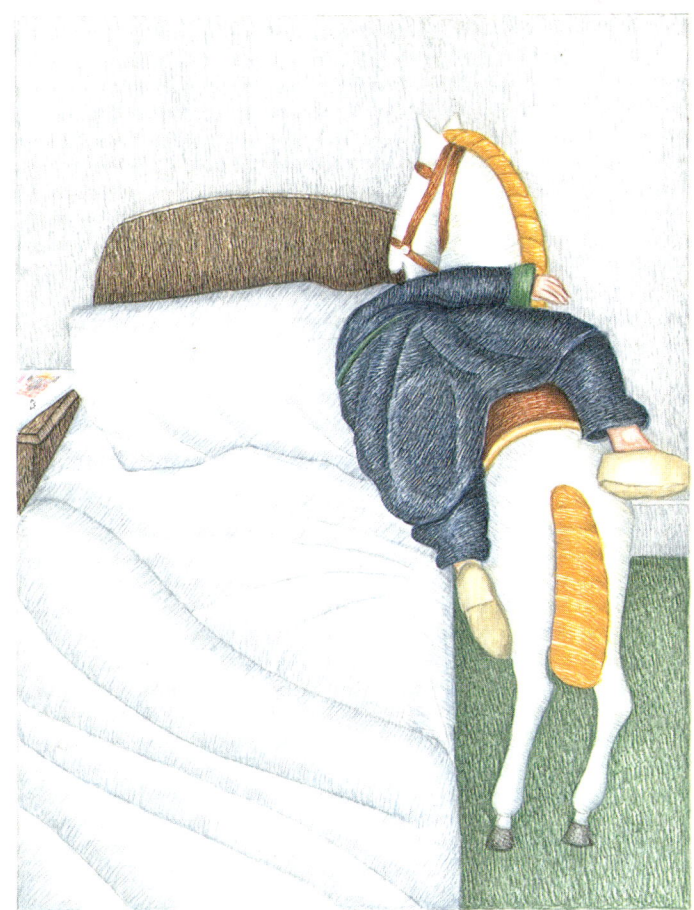